Dear Family Members,

Just as your child grows incl
skills grow word by word. You
every word in this book because each one has its own special
page. This set-up will help your child learn that words and
pictures have meaning.

Your child will also come to understand an important concept
about how speech and print are different:

> Iloveyou—sounds like this.
> I love you—looks like this.

Concepts like this one help your child grow as a reader.
These skills, when combined with decoding and
understanding stories, will lead to reading success.

Remember, the most important part of family reading time
is in a word—YOU!

Happy Reading,

Francie Alexander
Chief Education Officer,
Scholastic Education

Three Tips to Get Started:

1. *Before* reading, look at the cover, and talk about what you
   will read together.
2. *During* reading, read each word and talk about the story.
3. *After* reading, let your child choose a favorite word and
   make a picture to illustrate it. You and your child can
   make your own word by word reader!

To all of the children who color inside,
or outside, of the lines.
—M.R.

Copyright © 2002 by Michael Rex.
All rights reserved. Published by Scholastic Inc.
SCHOLASTIC, WORD BY WORD FIRST READER, CARTWHEEL BOOKS, and
associated logos are trademarks and/or registered trademarks of Scholastic Inc.

Library of Congress Cataloging-in-Publication Data
Rex, Michael.
    Where can bunny paint? / by Michael Rex.
       p.   cm. — (Word by word first reader)
    Summary: After several failed attempts, Bunny finally gets to paint something.
    ISBN 0-439-36605-4 (pbk)
    [1. Rabbits—Fiction. 2. Painting—Fiction] I. Title. II. Series

    PZ7.R32875 We 2002
[E] — dc21   2001049146

10 9 8 7 6 5 4 3 2   02 03 04 05 06
Printed in the U.S.A.
First printing, April 2002

Where Can Bunny Paint?

by Michael Rex

Cartwheel BOOKS®

SCHOLASTIC INC.

New York   Toronto   London   Auckland   Sydney
Mexico City   New Delhi   Hong Kong   Buenos Aires

2004. 2.
실

Bunny.

Paint.

Brush.

Wall.

Sit.

Chicken.

Start.

No!

Go.

Follow.

Fence.

Start.

No!

Truck.

Start.

No!

Where?

Here!

Egg!

Yellow.

Stripes.

Blue.

Zigzags.

Pink.

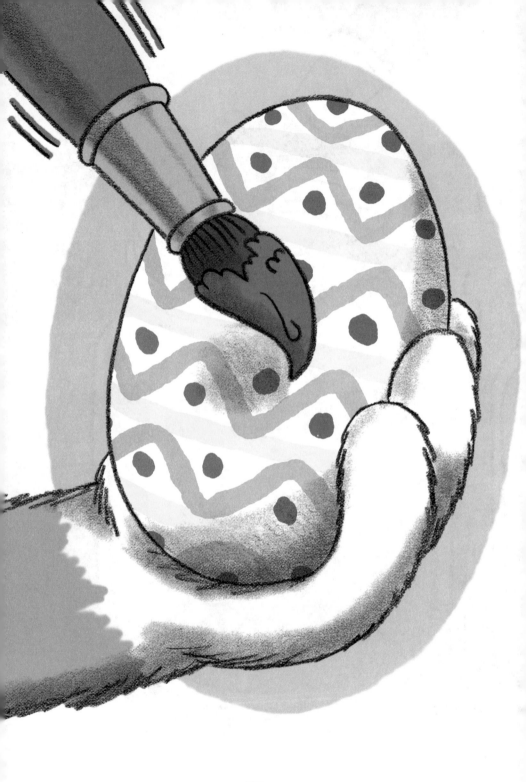

Dots.

Watch.

Done!

Clap.

Thanks!